Hattie
and the Fox

by Mem Fox
Illustrated by Patricia Mullins

SCHOLASTIC INC.

New York Toronto London Auckland Sydney

Hattie was a big black hen.
One morning she looked up and said,
"Goodness gracious me!
I can see a nose in the bushes!"

3

"Good grief!" said the goose.
"Well, well!" said the pig.

"Who cares?" said the sheep.
"So what?" said the horse.
"What next?" said the cow.

6

8

And Hattie said,
"Goodness gracious me!
I can see a nose
and two eyes in the bushes!"

"Good grief!" said the goose.
"Well, well!" said the pig.
"Who cares?" said the sheep.
"So what?" said the horse.
"What next?" said the cow.

12

And Hattie said,
"Goodness gracious me!
I can see a nose, two eyes,
and two ears in the bushes!"

"Good grief!" said the goose.
"Well, well!" said the pig.
"Who cares?" said the sheep.
"So what?" said the horse.
"What next?" said the cow.

14

16

And Hattie said,
"Goodness gracious me!
I can see a nose, two eyes, two ears,
and two legs in the bushes!"

"Good grief!" said the goose.
"Well, well!" said the pig.
"Who cares?" said the sheep.
"So what?" said the horse.
"What next?" said the cow.

And Hattie said,
"Goodness gracious me!
I can see a nose, two eyes, two ears, two legs,
and a body in the bushes!"

"Good grief!" said the goose.
"Well, well!" said the pig.
"Who cares?" said the sheep.
"So what?" said the horse.
"What next?" said the cow.

And Hattie said,
"Goodness gracious me!
I can see a nose, two eyes, two ears, a body, four legs,
and a tail in the bushes!
It's a fox! It's a fox!"
And she flew very quickly into a nearby tree.

"Oh, no!" said the goose.
"Dear me!" said the pig.
"Oh, dear!" said the sheep.
"Oh, help!" said the horse.

But the cow said, "MOO!"

so loudly that the fox was frightened and ran away.

And they were all so surprised
that none of them said anything
for a very long time.

Text copyright © 1986 by Mem Fox.
Illustrations copyright © 1986 by Patricia Mullins.
All rights reserved. Published by Scholastic Inc., 555 Broadway,
New York, NY 10012, by arrangement with
Simon & Schuster Children's Publishing Division.
Printed in the U.S.A.
ISBN 0-590-67896-5

2   3   4   5   6   7   8   9   10   08   02   01   00   99   98